Disney
CLUB PENGUIN™

COMICS

VOLUME 1

GROSSET & DUNLAP
Published by the Penguin Group
Penguin Group (USA) Inc., 375 Hudson Street, New York, New York 10014, USA
Penguin Group (Canada), 90 Eglinton Avenue East, Suite 700,
Toronto, Ontario M4P 2Y3, Canada
(a division of Pearson Penguin Canada Inc.)
Penguin Books Ltd., 80 Strand, London WC2R ORL, England
Penguin Group Ireland, 25 St. Stephen's Green, Dublin 2, Ireland
(a division of Penguin Books Ltd.)
Penguin Group (Australia), 250 Camberwell Road,
Camberwell, Victoria 3124, Australia
(a division of Pearson Australia Group Pty. Ltd.)
Penguin Books India Pvt. Ltd., 11 Community Centre,
Panchsheel Park, New Delhi–110 017, India
Penguin Group (NZ), 67 Apollo Drive, Rosedale,
North Shore 0632, New Zealand (a division of Pearson New Zealand Ltd.)
Penguin Books (South Africa) (Pty.) Ltd., 24 Sturdee Avenue,
Rosebank, Johannesburg 2196, South Africa

Penguin Books Ltd., Registered Offices:
80 Strand, London WC2R ORL, England

Library of Congress Control Number: 2009012535

ISBN 978-0-448-45182-4   10 9 8 7 6 5 4 3 2

WHAT DO YOU SUPPOSE THEY'RE SAYING?

HM? I DON'T KNOW. MAYBE THEY'RE SPEAKING IN ANOTHER LANGUAGE?

WELL, THEY'RE LESS CONFUSING THAN THE PENGUINS WHO ONLY TALK IN EXPRESSIONS.

?

WHY *THE CLUB PENGUIN TIMES* DOESN'T INCLUDE WEATHER REPORTS:
5-DAY FORECAST

THURSDAY

FRIDAY

SATURDAY

SUNDAY

MONDAY

HEY, WHAT'S GOING ON?

WHY AREN'T YOU DRESSED?

YEAH, IT'S THE MEDIEVAL PARTY!

I DIDN'T KNOW! I'LL HAVE SOMETHING *AWESOME* NEXT TIME, YOU GUYS.

AND SO...

FORSOOTH! YON— HEY! WHERE ARE ALL YOUR COSTUMES?

WHAT, FOR THE MEDIEVAL PARTY?

THAT ENDED, LIKE, YESTERDAY.

YEAH. WE'RE ALL ABOUT THIS ROCK NOW.

AROUND CLUB PENGUIN

YOU LOOK TIRED! HARD DAY?

YOU HAVE NO IDEA.

WHEW! STARTED THIS MORNING WITH A CREW OF DRILLERS AT THE ICEBERG, BUT THEN THERE WAS THIS BUNCH OF ROBOTS WHO BROKE US UP AND I GOT TURNED *INTO* A ROBOT.

SO I WAS WANDERING AROUND WITH THE OTHER ROBOTS, AND THEN A *CHEERLEADER* CHASED US ALL AWAY. CAN YOU BELIEVE THAT? *ONE* CHEERLEADER. ROBOTS THESE DAYS.

GOODNESS!

ANYWAY! AFTER AN AFTERNOON OF MAKING CANDY PIZZAS, I JUST NEEDED TO COME IN FOR A CUP OF COFFEE. AFTER THIS, I'VE GOT TO GO DIRECT A PLAY AT THE STAGE!

SOUNDS LIKE A FULL DAY!

MAYBE YOU SHOULD GIVE UP . . . ?

IT'LL TIP!

PUFFLES, PUFFLES, PUFFLES

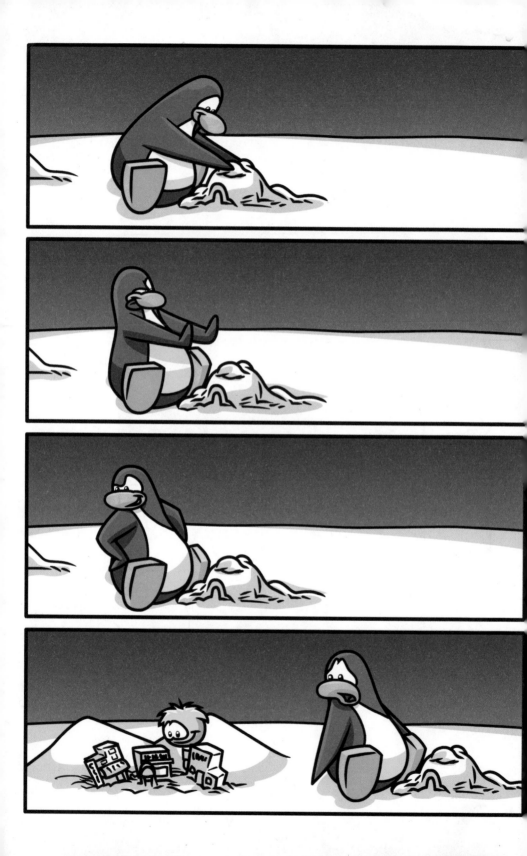

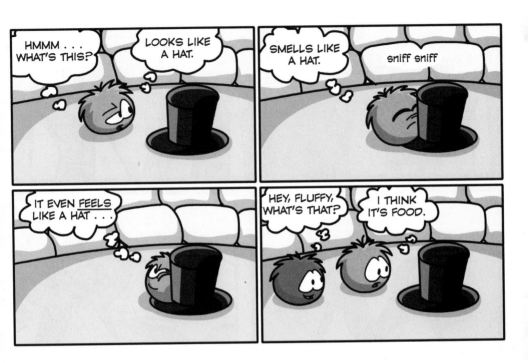

It's been a week since I've tried to infiltrate puffle society.

I don't think I've learned anything yet, but I refuse to give up. I still don't even know how they communicate.

All they seem to do is just sit around... smiling at each other.

I think I've wasted a week of my life.

FAMOUS FRIENDS

GARY'S FAILED DESIGNS

SKI LIFT 1000

TOASTER 1000

ORANGE JUICE 1000

WELL, HEY! GOOD TO SEE YOU ALL.

WHY DON'T WE START WITH YOU GUYS SHOWING ME YOUR MOVES?

WOW . . .

WE'VE, UH, GOT A LOT OF WORK AHEAD OF US.

SENSEI! PLEASE SHARE WITH US YOUR WISDOM.

The wisest penguin knows every journey begins with a single step.

And that it's easy to sound very wise if you say things in haiku.

...

YOU GOT THAT FROM A FORTUNE COOKIE, DIDN'T YOU?

...

NINJA VANISH!

POOF!

ALL FUN
AND GAMES

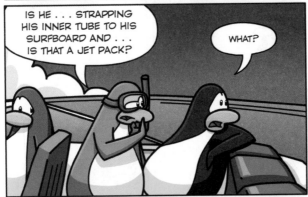